STEP ON IT, ANDREW

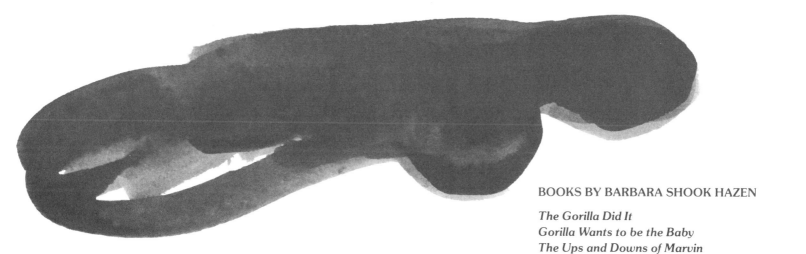

BOOKS BY BARBARA SHOOK HAZEN

The Gorilla Did It
Gorilla Wants to be the Baby
The Ups and Downs of Marvin
Why Couldn't I Be and Only Kid Like You, Wigger

BOOKS BY LISL WEIL

Donkey Head
Gillie and the Flattering Fox
The Very First Story Ever Told
Esther

STEP ON IT, ANDREW

Story by

BARBARA SHOOK HAZEN

Pictures by LISL WEIL

Atheneum   New York   1980

LIBRARY OF CONGRESS CATALOGING IN PUBLICATION DATA

Hazen, Barbara Shook.
  Step on it, Andrew.

  SUMMARY: Andrew's mother is in a hurry and
asks him to step on it, which he does, with
interesting results.
  [1. Mud—Fiction]   I. Weil, Lisl.
II. Title.
PZ7.H314975St   [E]   80-12522
ISBN 0-689-30792-6

Published simultaneously in Canada by
McClelland & Stewart, Ltd.
Printed by The Connecticut Printers, Inc.
Hartford, Connecticut
Bound by A. Horowitz & Sons/Bookbinders, Inc.
Fairfield, New Jersey
First Edition

One day
Andrew's mother
was in a big hurry.
She was running late,
and she didn't want to miss
the light, because the Super Mart
was about to close, and she didn't
have anything for dinner,
and so she called out,
"Step on it, Andrew."
And Andrew did.

2111337

Mother: I'm running behind.
Andrew: I'm running behind you.

He really stepped on it,
right on the middle
of a magnificent mud puddle.

Mother: Andrew,
what are you doing?
Andrew: You told me to!

He stepped on it so hard
thick blobs of mud
splattered his slicker
and blotted out the daisies
on his mother's best coat.

Mother: I just got it back from
the cleaner's.
Andrew: I'm sorry.

He stepped on it so hard
globs of mud
shot into the greengrocer's
and coated
all the rutabagas and radishes
and seven varieties of bean sprouts
with brown ooze.

Greengrocer: Somebody's a gonna pay for this!

He stepped on it so hard
a shower of mud
splattered a group of striking sanitation workers
and made the ink on their protest posters run.

Union Leader: Now City Hall's slinging mud at us.

He stepped on it so hard
a salvo of mud
shot into the Last National Bank,
between the granite columns
and behind the teller's window,
and knocked the rubber gun
out of a masked man's hand
right in the middle of a bank robbery.

Robber: Don't shoot. I surrender.

He stepped on it so hard
missiles of mud
cascaded into the open fourth-floor windows
of the *Daily Grind* and

ruined the afternoon edition,
which was just coming
off press.

Editor: Stop the presses!
Pressman: They are stopped, you dummy.

Mayor: Here's mud in your eye!
Councilman: Another one of the mayor's cheap shots.

He stepped on it so hard
a fountain of mud
sprayed the roof garden of the Grandiron building,
where the mayor had been playing
a game of sticky wickets
with the town council.

All the while

Artist: Help! Fire!

a flash fire was raging
out of control
in the artist's loft
just next to it,
which the firemen couldn't
reach by conventional means
because the ladder
was too rickety
because the town council
hadn't voted funds
for modern equipment
because they were mad
at the mayor
for not stepping in
to stop the sanitation
workers' strike.

Fortunately,
Andrew stepped on it so exceedingly hard
that the force of that fountain of mud
completely snuffed out the flames

just in time
for the greengrocer to wash
his rutabagas and radishes,
and for the mayor to be rescued,

and the slippery robber
to be put in jail,
and the councilmen
to change their minds,
and the sanitation workers
to change their vote
and go back on the job,
and the artist
to put up a fire-sale sign.

Worker: It's our duty to clean up our town.
Worker: What this dump needs is a clean sweep.

Editor: What a story!
Worker: What a mess.

And the editor-in-chief to
change the headline on the late edition.

And after all that, the Super Mart was closed.

So everyone,
except the stalwart sanitation workers,
went home and
took nice hot, soaky baths,
to be squeaky clean for the big banquet

Andrew: Ahhh!

in honor of quick-thinking Andrew,
who did as he was asked
when he really stepped on it.

HURRAH FOR ANDREW

It was all Mom's fault for making me.

in honor of quick-thinking Andrew,
who did as he was asked
when he really stepped on it.

HURRAH FOR ANDREW

It was all Mom's fault for making me.